First U.S. edition 1992
First published in Great Britain in 1992 by
Walker Books Ltd., London.
Library of Congress Catalog Card Number 91-58740
Library of Congress Cataloging-in-Publication Data
Su, Lucy, 1948-
Jinzi and Minzi at the playground / by Lucy Su.
— 1st U.S. ed. — (A Candlewick toddler book)
"First published in Great Britain in 1992 by
Walker Books, Ltd., London" — T.p. verso.
Summary: Two kittens enjoy the slide, wading pool,
merry-go-round, and swings at the playground.
ISBN 1-56402-052-5 : $5.95
[1. Cats—Fiction.   2. Play—Fiction.] I. Title. II. Series.
PZ7.S9432Jj 1992   91-58740
[E]—dc20

10 9 8 7 6 5 4 3 2 1

Printed in Hong Kong

Candlewick Press
2067 Massachusetts Avenue
Cambridge, Massachusetts 02140

Jinzi and Minzi
at the Playground
by Lucy Su

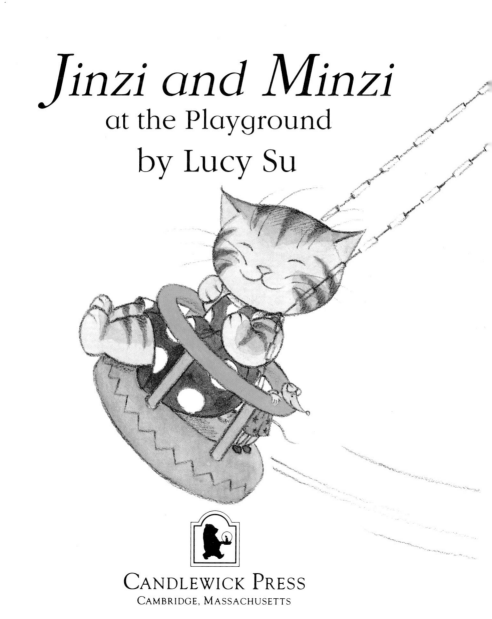

CANDLEWICK PRESS
CAMBRIDGE, MASSACHUSETTS

Jinzi and Minzi
are at the playground.

Jinzi and Minzi
go around and around
on the merry-go-round...

and in the wading pool.

Jinzi and Minzi go up
and down on the slide…

and on the jungle gym.

Jinzi and Minzi go to and fro
on the horse and the giraffe…

and on the swings.

And after all that
it's time for lunch!